The Island Of Nestra

Part Two

By Simon Delaney

ABOUT THE AUTHOR

The author grew up on a small estate and has faced numerous challenges throughout life, including learning difficulties, anxiety, depression, and other mental health struggles. For many years, they believed they weren't capable of achieving anything significant. However, with the support of Authors Solution UK, they discovered their potential and realised their goals. Once the book is published, the author plans to donate a copy to the NCHA project, where they once lived, to inspire others and show that no matter the obstacles, it's possible to achieve your dreams.

DEDICATION

To my family – my mum, my four sisters, nieces, nephews, and to Sky – for being the unwavering support that has guided me through every step of this journey. Growing up on a small estate, I faced many challenges, including learning difficulties and mental health struggles, and I often doubted my own potential. However, your love and encouragement showed me that anything is possible, and for that, I am forever grateful.

SPECIAL THANKS

To Authors Solution UK – thank you for providing the resources and support that allowed me to turn my dreams into reality. This book is proof that, despite any struggles or self-doubt, one can still reach their goals. I am honored to donate a copy to the NCHA Project, where I once lived, as a reminder that no matter the challenges, success is within reach.

Many years later....

Winter falls like gentile snowflakes gracing your cheek. Blanketing roofs in a white sheet that shines in the dark.

Boats slide across the ice as fishing is the future. Instead, they bash holes into the ice, waiting for the fish to come up for air as they spear them and drag them out of the water.

Trade routes are cut off as the ice is too thick to sail threw, leaving the island cut off from the rest of the world.

Unable to trade farms or do much of anything, the villagers have fun building snowmen and having snowball fights with their kids.

Many days pass before the snow starts to melt again, and they are able to set their feet back on their boats again.

Clear sailing ahead...

Sailing on the melting fractured ice, it is plain sailing ahead as traders are seen venturing once again to the island.

Stores now at the ready, once covered in snow, are now clear and full of goods awaiting the traders in the distance.

Later that day...

A sudden thick cloud hangs over the village. Unsure what to think at first, they stand clueless, looking around above their heads, trying to figure it out.

Unsure what's happening, until lightning strikes trees violently at a distance, setting them on fire and sending them crashing to the ground.

As deafening thunder echoes loudly threw the dark cloud, thunder roars like gods scorned, waring above their heads.

Afraid, they scatter around like ants in the rain. Confused and scared, they head for the church.

Mass panic...

A mad dash ensues, trying to be the first, pushing and shoving, fighting their way threw the crowds of people.

All are trying to be the first in out of the freakish weather, pushing people out of the way, knocking each other over in the panic.

The elderly and young are pushed and knocked out of the way in the heat of the moment, leaving them injured and trampled on the floor. Finally, after some commotion, they are all in the church praying to the gods for forgiveness and help stores left abandoned to the elements and potential thieves. They await for the dark storm to pass, winds blow violently, hitting the walls and roof of the church, thinking the church will be destroyed, curl up on the floor, holding hands and praying to be saved.

Thinking it's a bad omen, they have never seen anything like it before in the history of the island.

Threw the eye of a dying storm... but as quickly as it came, the fleeting clouds left the sky clear as they took a moment to compose themselves, making sure everyone was ok.

The whole village in good spirits, cheers and chants, hail the gods, thinking they answered their prayers.

They start to leave the church, heading back to their places of work. Stepping outside, the blinding sun nocks them back.

They notice a few straw karts have been knocked over and pottery smashed into pieces on the floor.

As it could have been much worse, they were grateful their homes were still in one piece, fearing all would be lost.

Unfortunately, the stores are ruined as they have been blown over, and their goods are left lying everywhere.

Trade route blocked...

They can be seen just beyond the trees blocking the way, and a real mess is left by the storm, sparing nothing preventing the karts and people access to and from the village trade route, devastated by the loss of trade caused by it.

But luckily, the villagers are grateful that the whole woodland didn't catch fire, spreading to their villages and homes.

Trying to move the trunks and branches of the trees from the road together, they are unable to move them alone.

Struggling to drag the trees or the branches out of the way, the frustrated villagers give up and return back to the village.

Specialists are summoned...

Woodcutters are despatched to the trade root to cut and clear the burnt and broken trees blocking the road.

Getting to work on the fallen trees takes a lot of woodcutters using primitive saws to cut threw the trees.

Cutting them into smaller, more manageable pieces, they dragged them away from the path and left at the side of the road.

It was anything but light work to remove the trees blocking the way with their primitive saws and manpower it didn't take too long.

They set fire to the trees that have fallen, reducing them to charcoal to use for different things back in the village.

They haul the large amount of charcoal that is recovered from the burnt trees back to the village.

They supply it to the local market for people to use in their homes to keep fires going and to sterilise wounds.

With the road now cleared and reopened, the way for the karts and people is now ready to go threw.

Spoiled goods...

Thankful the trade route is back up and running the village trade routes can now resume as normal, returning back to their stores.

Picking the goods from off the floor, rescuing what they can, throwing away the food that's been ruined.

Setting their stores back up from off the floor, collect the wood planks that rest on small mudbrick walls. Beautiful clothing is covered with dirt, ruined, blown violently everywhere, scattered around in the wind.

Luckily the jewels and strong barrels full of alcohol are still able to be saved. Picking them up places them back in the stores.

Buckets of grain blown over and spilled out upon the ground, ruined by the wind, as the grains mixed with dirt, becoming no longer edible bottles of their finest drink, are also nocked everywhere, but fortunately, none of them were broken, just scattered everywhere on the floor.

They send someone to collect labourers to bring more goods to replace the ones that have been ruined.

It took a while to gather enough workers with karts to help them as they needed. Else, were have just a skeleton crew at work camps.

Cleaning and restocking...

Some helpers who finish their previous jobs are dispatched straight away with karts to help the market replenish their stock.

With a lot of hard work and pulling countless karts, dropping the new off, and sweeping and clearing the floor up of the old goods, the villagers soon fill up their stores again like nothing ever happened. The help summoned also tidied up and disposed of the old goods.

Traders return...

Just in time, as a few traders seem to be coming to the island after the freak storm, eager to trade, they await for them to arrive on the beach with their boats.

Welcoming them to the island with a heartfelt handshake they help the traders with their goods off their boats.

Trade begins straight away, going back and forth with items, trying to come to a deal acceptable for both sides.

Many luxury jewels and jewellery were brought, offsetting the loss of the ruined goods. A great day was had by all.

As time goes on and more traders come to the island, the villagers start to worry just how many traders they can acomadate on the island.

Having only small stores in a small part of the island, they can't keep their eye on everyone who comes to the village.

Threats from outsiders...

With potential threats that could come to the island, security needs to be put in place for their safety and everyone else's.

With new threats on the horizon, armed scout parties with swords in their belts are dispatched to patrol the ends of the island to keep everyone safe.

They soon have problems with poachers traveling to the island to steal the local's wild food supply, and people are needed to keep them away.

Poachers descend...

Just missing them by a fraction of time seems to always miss them but notice what routes they take and decide to hide there.

Hoping they will come back, just sit there hiding and waiting for them to come back, and after a short time they can be seen coming back.

Poachers arrested...

Poachers descend upon the island beach once again, but this time, they are waiting, catching them in the act, swoop in.

Scaring them half to death as they jump out from hiding, they freeze, too scared to move with swords pointed at their throats.

Tying up their hands, march them back to the village in single file, blindfolded so they could see where they were going. They were pushed and thrown to the ground, only allowing them to their knees to take off their blindfolds. The light is strong as they try to refocus their sight.

They were put on a quick trial for being caught poaching and found guilty straight away by a unanimous jury.

The law of the land...

The sentencing made clear what the punishment would be for the elders of the village, and they acted out as ordered to make sure they never came back. Some were against the punishment, but the elders have spoken and can't be overruled, or they will be held in contempt.

The punishment was harsh for the poachers. Some were whipped, others were stripped naked and paraded, and the rest had bad fruit and food thrown at them.

Completely degraded, they are kicked to the ground as they try and make their escape, trying to get back to their feet.

They are followed as villagers throw stones at them and laugh at them as they stumble, making it closer to the shore.

They don't have much time to take their boats and escape, away from the onslaught of villagers chasing after them.

Seeing them rowing away, they know they won't be back again, making an example out of them so no others come back, allowing them to spread the message. The villagers were a bit harsh, but they had to send a message that people couldn't come and steal from their island with no consequence.

To make sure it never happens again, the elders put together a group of scouts to walk the shoreline in groups, one in each direction, to span the island.

Enemies spotted...

Being despatched to make sure no one comes back, one spot ships off in the distance on the far side of the island whilst patrolling the shores, sending someone to warn the villagers by horseback. To alert them there might be trouble on the way. Approaching the island and nearly making it back in the heat of the moment, the messenger falls off his horse, running for the village, alerting the villagers of what they saw in the distance. Panic hits the village as everyone starts running for somewhere to hide. Jars were knocked over stores broken, a lot of damage done in the madness of it all, people tripping over stuff, falling over, total chaos.

Traders flee...

Hearing the message, the merchants are suddenly spooked. They drop what they're doing, start to flee quickly, leaving all the goods that they brought behind and quickly make their escape back to their boats.

They dump the excess goods they brought with them that didn't get loaded onto the island into the sea as they return back to their ships.

Quickly packing up their stores, the rest make haste back to the village, karts packed high and overflowing.

As they head back to the village, it would appear they are coming straight in for the attack. They take cover in their homes. Soldiers are summoned immediately to the spot where the attackers were last seen coming towards them in a hurry.

Ready for battle...

Most fresh from the academy, having trained hard in many forms of combat all day and every day, begin to get ready for battle.

Standing strong, the soldiers and the volunteer villagers march information to the side of the island confidently with swords, shields and armour, ready and waiting for a great battle.

Loud chanting and banging of shields get themselves worked up and ready for a bloody end for the attackers

with the gods watching over them, the soldiers are fearless standing strong in position continue to bang their swords against their shields as enemies storm the beach.

Battle begins...

The attackers out outnumbered, carrying only crude weapons that broke as the soldiers' swords cut threw them very easily, shooting arrows from afar. As they make their way onto the island, the soldiers kneel down and lift up their shields as the arrows hit, doing no damage.

Rising up, they charge the attackers head-on, and swords clash. As the battle begins, they cut threw them easily as their blood-soaked bodies litter the beach.

All the enemies lay dying, sprawled out all over the beach, as they take their last breath before closing their eyes.

Quick victory...

The enemy came ill-prepared, and their cost with inferior weapons and fight tactics were no match for the veteran soldiers.

Slaying the enemy without a problem, laughing at them, mocking the dead, an easy battle is fought, still with plenty of energy.

Spoils of war...

After the soldiers begin to pile up the dead from the beach and waterline, putting them in a pile, set fire to them.

Leaving their superior boats behind them, the soldiers have an idea to transform them into fishing boats, dragging them back to the boat yard and taking them out to the sea. Row their way to the ship, taking a small army with them in case anyone was aboard. Boarding the large ship, totally empty, they secure it, take it, and set sail to the island for their villagers and soldiers to use.

Now they have something to work off. They can make their own ships powered by sails instead of man powered, a leap forward in technology for them.

No longer need helpers to power the boats and ships, they implement sails onto all their ships and boats.

Returning triumphant...

A few casualties are laid with their swords and shields on their new boats and taken back to the village for a proper funeral.

Returning to the village, triumphant, they are greeted by celebrating villagers awaiting their return as news of their victory has reached the village.

Very pleased with themselves, the soldiers return to their camp for more hard training, eager to get even better than before, becoming a force to be reckoned with.

The few that were lost are quickly replaced with more eager new recruits proud to be a soldier, who turn up in a crowd, waiting in a line to sign up.

Advanced boats....

The boatyards are instructed to make trade boats with sails so they can travel to different places and explore on the wind. Instead of human-powered, the smaller boats are made very quickly with sails that work well for fishing as they no longer have to use a paddle, scaring the fish away. The trade boats take a while to build, using up a lot of wood and man hours to complete, placing it on log rollers and slowly rolling it out to sea line.

Rolling it into the water, everyone pushes it into deeper water until it clears off the beach and puts the Anker down so it doesn't float away.

Out at sea...

loading it with goods using smaller boats to reach it are soon ready for departure filled with food and drink.

Knowing they could be months at sea, they prepare everything they need for the long voyage ahead of them: food, drink and other supplies.

They are gone for months, traveling the seas to new places, trading and buying until their boats are full return back to the shore of the island.

Back to the island...

With many goods, they unpack the trading boats and they are greeted with small boats to collect the bounty they brought back. They are welcomed back like heroes back from long overseas combat, bringing a lot of new and unusual goods with them.

Before setting back out for more trading with far-off places that wouldn't normally be accessible otherwise as they are too far away to reach them to trade themselves, the world is a large place, and many delights can be traded in far-off places with many different cultures.

Very excited, the traders embark on a great adventure into unknown lands with many goods to buy and sell.

Advanced housing...

Being isolated with only a handful of traders, their tribe hasn't been able to evolve and grow until now. On their way from the island, they open a close trade route that will allow them to build better houses with stone instead of mudbrick and straw.

Breaking out of an old kingdom into a new era of stone. Replacing the outdated huts with new ones.

A lot of jewels, fine clothing and drinks are traded for the small stone blocks dragged by boat onto the shore, where it's pilled up on the beach, ready for collection.

Collecting the materials...

Villagers with karts soon make their way to the beach to collect the stone, loading the karts up to transport it back to the village ready for building.

With heavy karts, the labourers struggle to push it back threw the sand to the village as their wheels start to suffer under the strain of the load. Horses were tied to the front of the karts to help with the weight, dragging it threw the sand, making it a lot easier, taking four people to move one kart with horses, more people are needed to transport the stone quicker to the village.

Returning to the beach with karts and horses soon makes it a lot easier to move the stone than a few blocks of stone per person.

Many blocks were collected from the beach as delivery was very slow from the traders to deliver to the island.

Meanwhile, patiently await a lot more stones to reach them and continue to trade their goods with other traders.

It takes a few weeks and many trade boats to gather enough stone to start building luxury new homes.

In the meantime it is stored in the village in the space at the back of huts to keep safe, away from passing boats that might see it as fair game to steal.

As it starts to pile up behind the villager's huts, they become concerned about it toppling onto their houses, destroying them a strong wind could mean a lot of villagers could become homeless as the heavy stone will destroy their homes.

New homes....

One at a time, the old mud brick houses are dismantled and disposed of as new houses are slowly built, freeing up some space behind the villager's huts.

With stone masons needed a group of skilled construction workers and labourers to begin to build houses stone by stone, one house at a time.

Construction is slow as labourers are needed elsewhere, and there are only a few on hand. It takes all day to lay every stone.

Wood is placed slanted down the roof in tiles so the rain runs off each one instead of into the villager's houses.

A great idea...

the boat makers have an idea: to coat the roofs with a kind of glue used to seal their boats to make them waterproof. The black goop is thick and slimy but goes on a treat as it seals over the wood, protecting it from the elements.

It takes a long time and resources to gather enough workers for every villager's home. Building two or three a day speeds up construction.

Woodworkers decide to make new tables, chairs and beds for the villagers beautifully crafted in the best wood available.

With the new village starting to take shape, the villagers are very happy with their new homes, treated wood flooring placed on the floor instead of dirt.

Another luxury is made, a brand new sweeping brush made of wood and straw bristles for the house floors to keep them tidy.

Overseas battles...

Trouble from a faraway trade village is under attack and needs reinforcements, as news reaches the island, from desperate traders.

Wanting to help them out with their problem, they assign soldiers to be dispatched to the trader's location. Soldiers quickly board their boats, dragging them down the beach, reaching the sea as they set sail to the trader's island.

Bad weather ahead...

Whilst at sea, a storm hits, and waves wash up against the boats, knocking them around and drenching the soldiers.

Fighting against the powerfull winds to guide their boats in the right direction, hoping they not be knocked off course.

Everyone gets involved, trying to point the sail in the right direction so they don't get lost at sea or worse.

Hoping their boats down, turning over, dumping them into the sea, trying to keep them balanced, a hard battle against the waves to keep them upright continues.

Disembarking....

Under terrible weather, only three out of four reach the island, as they were lost during the storm disembarking and pulling their boats onto the sandy beach, and take out the swords and shields ready for battle, avenging their lost brothers taken by the sea by destroying the enemy as brutally as possible seeing a prospect of a great battle charge towards the fighting, but they pause confused on who to attack.

Confused...

Disorientated by the storm, it takes a while for them to gain their exposure. Standing on the beach, noticing the fight going off not far in front of them, they scratch their heads, not knowing who to fight, unable to decide who to attack. A passing village trader sees them on the beach and points to them what side to fight with.

Heading into the eye of the battle, they raise their swords and shields and head towards the enemy without fear.

Out for blood...

Ready, they march together as one to attack the enemy. Creeping up behind them lands a death blow, killing them instantly.

Taking them by surprise as they are preoccupied with the villagers makes a great strategy. Before they notice anything, they get the upper hand on them. They violently hack and slash away threw their weapons and armour, with ease, as they fall to the ground, take them out with no remorse.

Swords and shields clash violently as they fight Perseus, and their advanced weapons and armour soon become apparent. Out maned they still fight hard, slaying them, swords and shields flying everywhere. As the attackers start to fall, thinning them out, only thirty soldiers against many with their superior training kicks in, fighting as one instead of a separate divided army.

Seeing how the outsiders fight, the trader's army is inspired to fight harder, trying to keep up with overseas soldiers.

A well-fought battle...

Bodies of their enemies lay everywhere on the ground, with none left behind to escape back to their boats.

Stopping anyone from escaping home and calling for back up to bring way more soldiers to attack with.

The battle is soon won as the last of the attackers fall by their swords, and the village soldiers are left in shock.

Not knowing what to do with all their bodies and blood all over the beach, send labourers to shovel the blood off the beach the best way they can.

Berrial at sea...

The trader's village loads the bodies onto boats. It takes a lot of boats for them all, but they get started taking them out to sea, dumping their dead bodies into the water far away, food for the aquatic creatures to feast on.

A lot of sharks are quickly attracted to the boats, and they can smell the blood as they dump the enemy bodies into the sea.

Attracted by the blood in the water, the sharks circle the boat for a while until they dump their bodies into the water.

The sharks go into a feeding frenzy, ripping chunks out and devouring them as the sharks fight amongst themselves over the food.

Their fins can be seen coming to the surface, dragging the bodies under the water, never to be seen again.

Their blood colors the sea red around their boat, as there are many sharks around in a feeding frenzy, fighting amongst themselves for food.

A harsh way to go, made even worse if they were alive, but they have nowhere to dispose of the bodies, so it's their only way.

They flee the area before the sharks start to attack the boats, knocking them into the water and eating them alive.

Returning back to the shore emptied of enemies, disembark their ships and regreet the overseas soldiers.

A new ally...

Seeing how they struggled in battle, they decided to help them to be better soldiers with better weapons imported to them.

They set up a trade route and came to an arrangement to supply them with better shields, swords and armour.

They introduce themselves as the Jetou clan. They are very thankful for helping them out and offer goods in return for the weapons and armour.

The army decides to leave a soldier behind to train the Jetou army so they are able to fight better without fear.

With the best-trained army around, not letting up in training, fight hard and are recognised for helping and dispatching the enemy so easily and quickly.

Dialog of attackers...

The enemy attacks many villagers, taking all their supplies like gold, jewels and anything else worth anything.

They tell them of an island far away full of greedy people who will attack any village, stealing everything they have.

The traders plead to them, warning them never to go there as it will bring war upon their village and even destruction.

They go on to tell them the village is called Rhyjak and they should stay away from this island, describing the island to them as an island surrounded by jagged rocks placed around the island to damage and sink boats that don't know the area, praying on them and their cargo a map of that area was given showing were the island they should stay away from, showing were all the submerged, hidden rocks are.

A lot of places have heard the news of them helping Jetou, and their curiosity brings them to the island to see the soldiers that defeated the attacking army.

Back to business...

They ask how the soldiers could dispatch trained killers very easily without breaking a sweat and ask for military assistance.

They stay and travel to the soldier's camp, where they spend a lot of time observing and taking notes, but notes alone aren't good enough to fight a war. They ask to trade for some weapons and armour to help them along, as the villagers have superior weapons. Their trade is accepted, but they have one more condition: they can leave a soldier behind to learn from the best.

New recruits...

Agreeing, the soldier is soon recruited and begins training in the hope he can take back the training he has learned to train their own soldiers.

Many more follow, filling the camp to bursting with all these different villagers, leaving one behind, but luckily, the training is outside and in the woodland; in return, they would buy a lot more merchandise and trade, as well as blueprints for better trade ships powered threw wind and sails instead manpower.

Very excited with the prospects of more trade with new items they had never seen or heard before being brought to the island, the good times didn't last long as an armada of ships appeared on the horizon heading for the island.

Revenge of the fallen....

With the flags of the same ships that they beat in combat, they know they are coming in for revenge on their fallen soldiers.

Somehow, someone has tipped them off to the location of the soldiers that killed their army so quickly, maybe a lone trader hearing about the victory, caught in their snare, washed up on the rocks around the island, plundered and enslaved.

Out for revenge, one can hear the shouting on the boats from the shores. An angry army approaches closely. Scouts are sent to gather information on how many combatants there are that disembark off smaller ships onto the beach.

One hundred soldiers storm up the beach, unable to confront them as they're lured into the woods, where the soldiers train and hide.

At one with nature...

Poised for combat, they are ready for them using the woodland overgrowth to conceal themselves. Simple traps are set that would be set for poachers snaring them; they conceal them and wait for them to step on them.

In their element, they no every part of the woods, where the traps are, looking for the best part to hide and pick them off a few at a time.

Picking them off, attacking the last attacker that falls behind at a time, they soon start to slowly pick them off.

Frustrated, the army grows angrier, slashing at ghosts that attack and then disappear into the woods, ready for more.

One with nature...

The large forest hides a lot of soldiers spread out inside it, all taking key positions as they do in training, almost invincible like ghosts appear and disappear quickly, attacking the enemy and returning into the woods.

Hiding amongst the trees and behind bushes, the enemy is attacked in all directions, picking off the soldiers.

The woods are vast and can hide many soldiers amongst its vegetation. Knowing every part of it gives them the edge in battle, leading the enemy to the slaughter.

Before they realise it, half their soldiers have been killed, and the attackers go into formation, facing every side waiting for the next attack.

Sixty soldiers against fifty lure the enemy out of the woods and onto the beach, where they face them head-on.

Final stand...

After most of the army was defeated, a glorious victory was had. Never before have they faced such a large army.

With no casualties, the army stands tall with sixty men ready to lay their lives down to protect the village.

Sometimes, standing strong alone is better than an entire army. When they all stand alone together, ready to attack, the cowards flee back to their ships, defeated once again by the same army that dispatched them so easily.

Another small victory...

The soldier's spirits are high, and after the great defeat of the enemy almost double their size, they march back to camp very happy.

Think they're unbeatable; maybe they are on their own island, but there's a whole world out there where they don't have the same advantage.

Surprise attack...

Knowing the threats to other islands, they take the war to end it once and for all, gather many more soldiers from other lands as well and head to their island.

Many boats with a lot of soldiers make their way to the island, looking for payback for all the evil they have done to them.

They wait for nightfall and sneak into the camp; taking them by surprise, they gather them all up in the centre of their village.

Some of the soldiers claim the village as their own, as theirs were destroyed by them, and they have a better idea than execution.

Their treasures are taken and returned to their rightful owners, and some village soldiers are in an uproar, wanting to execute them.

With soldiers everywhere, there's no chance that they would win in battle against such odds; the cowards surrender.

A price to pay...

Surrounded in a circle around them, they sit powerless to do anything, awaiting their fates, thinking they will perish.

Instead, they get a pretty price for them as they sell them to a trader with armed guards to tie them up and lead them all away to their trade boat.

A fitting end for such evil people who live off the fear of others, killing men, women and children without remorse.

Seeing them tied up and taken away, the locals are in good spirits. They all come out to see their oppressors degraded, dragged and imprisoned like they were.

A new home...

With no interference from the remaining villagers, the traders stay behind, sending word to the rest of their people to come to their new home.

Spending a long time living on the open sea, the traders make their way to the island with haste to make it their own.

Bringing all the belongings they have with them, they disembark from their boats and reach the beach, unloading their goods. Their fellow traders greet them at the beach with a few locals to help carry their belongings into their new home.

A festival of joy...

A great celebration is thrown to celebrate their new home, with locals joining in, life is much better in the village.

With the evil defeated and dispelled forever, the locals no longer live in fear under the tyranny of their masters.

Knowing only pain and suffering under the old oppressors becomes a fresh breath of air for the locals, free at last, no longer slaves.

Spirits are high as men, women and children all enjoy the festivity thrown by their new settlers.

Bringing new luxuries to the island for all; instead of being poor and living in fear, food and drink were given to the poor to nourish them. Their island is rich in resources, and their farms are large and fertile, giving great yields of food, barley and flax.

With plenty of gems, gold and copper to extract, sticking out amongst the rocky areas, and much more.

The new settlers brought better industry with them, putting the people to work in their desired jobs to earn a living so they could buy food and other goods.

For the first time ever they are able to trade with different places freely, without fear of their masters.

Plundering old opperssors...

Raiding their oppressor's empty fortress, a lot of valuable treasures were found everywhere were found whilst demolishing it.

Plundering all its goods, selling them to traders at the market place. They get a a lot of gold for the treasures with a lot of goods. It gives them time to farm, dig for gems and establish better trade relations with their village.

Free at last...

No longer treated like slaves, they volunteer their services to work freely without distress or fear, removing the rocks around the island concealed in water so nobody runs shore onto them ever again.

It takes a few days, but the locals know where they all are, using rope to drag them onto the island, were people can take free of charge.

With a good job done and everyone set up now the soldiers embark onto their boats to return to Nestra, missing home.

Gathering all their weapons and goods, filling the boats up make their way to the beach, setting off across the water.

Troubled waters...

It's fine sailing until a black cloud envelopes the sky in darkness as lightning zig-zags threw the clouds.

Thundery clashes threw the heavens as waves rise, and their boats are battered by the strange weather.

The winds blow hard upon their sails, dragging the boats in the direction of the wind, powerless to stop it, brace themselves.

The boats rock back and forth, thinking the tide will capsize them, bracing themselves on whatever they can hold on to.

Not wanting to become shark food, they turn the boats and go with the wind, not knowing where it will take them nor wanting to perish in the ice cold water, with no way to make their escape in an emergency their victims of the storm.

Prayer to gods...

They say a little soldier's prayer whilst hanging on for dear life as the wind guides their way across the seas.

The sails start to come undone from their ropes blowing wildly around the boat, and the soldiers try to move the sail, covering their vision.

Compasses spin around like a tornado, still sailing blind threw the storm in darkness, and the crew becomes lost at sea.

With no way of knowing where they headed in the darkness, they were at the mercy of the sea, tying their sails back the way there was.

Storm passess...

Many hours pass lost at sea with taking so much water on board, they try to scoop up the water in buckets.

Throwing it overboard all together, helping soon empty the boat as best they can, looking at where they drifted to.

They have no chance of ever returning to their island or homes or seeing their loved ones ever again.

Thinking of their loved ones, they daydream about them, trying to take the attention off of being lost at sea.

They drift for a long time further and further out to see, blindly being blown by the wind on their sails drifting in unknown waters; they are wary of where they will end up as they see an island off in the distance.

Attack from under....

When something big rocks, their boats, almost falling out, remain quiet in case theres sharks under their boats.

Rising slowly from the depths of the sea, the soldiers look over the end of their boats to see what it is but see nothing in the murky water.

A giant seaworm attacks one of the boats, rocking it side to side as soldiers fall off and are devoured in its gaping mouth.

With a round gaping mouth and teeth so sharp it could cut a man in half, it attacks the side of the boat, breaking chunks out of it.

Its skin is too tough for swords to cut threw as they try to slash at it with no harm done to the creature.

The monster stands tall out of the sea with red piercing eyes and black scale plates layered like dragon skin.

The monster attacks...

Looking like it's touching the bottom, looks down upon the boat and starts to take people, swallowing them whole.

Grabbing hold of the soldiers, trying to harpoon them with its gaping mouth, flings them into the air, gulping them down.

Scared to death, having never seen such a thing like this before, panic, one soldier has a great idea to harm the creature.

Whilst trying to fend off the creature, they harpoon its body but have no effect, so they tie a sword to a stick and spear its mouth.

One for the team...

A soldier's bravery sacrifices himself to be taken holding the spear, spears it as he is swallowed into its mouth, stabbing it deep inside. Swallowing the makeshift spear, the creature cries out in pain thrashing around as it Cuts threw it from the inside out.

The soldier cuts his way back out just as it disappears back under the water, floating to the bottom, never to be seen again.

The soldiers regroup, leaving the damaged boat behind as there are fewer soldiers than there were before they see something in the distance; unsure what it could be, they head towards it before the giant sea worm comes back and attacks them.

A new island....

Reaching a strange island, they disembark their boats and explore the island, seeing a lot of weird venomous snakes, deadly lions and other wildlife.

Quietly tiptoe around them, slowly making their way through them without disturbing them, make their way into the overgrowth. They cut their way threw the overgrowth, knowing no one has travelled this path before feel a bit disheartened.

But after a while, they come across a village with a campfire lit in the middle of it; tired from all the walking, hungry and thirsty, they seek out nourishment.

A newfound village...

They enter the village, but no one is there; feeling something is wrong, the soldiers pull their swords and look around.

Seeing food is laid out on tables, knowing they must be around somewhere, they check their homes but see nothing; still seeing no one in the village or in the woodland, they decide to return back to the village to investigate a bit more.

Time to eat and drink...

Noticing the delicious food in the stores in the village, help themselves to it whilst quenching their thirst, with their bellies full and their thirst quenched and stomachs. They start to relax a little, putting their guard down, thinking no one around.

Return to the fire in the village to get warm as it's very cold surrounding it and sit by the fire, drying out their wet boots and other clothing.

Luck runs out...

When suddenly, they are surrounded by armed villagers appearing out of the woodland in complete camouflage. One minute, there was no one, then a load of armed villagers appeared out of no were sneak towards them, taking them off guard and by surprise, were defenceless against the armed villagers, surrounding them holding crossbows and spears, thinking the soldiers were going to attack them they force them to their knees with crossbows pointed at their heads, leaves them with no chance of pulling their weapons in defence.

Behind bars...

They are taken prisoner very quickly, being dragged to their feet are led to and locked up in a wooden cage, unable to escape.

Locked up without their weapons to defend themselves, they fear the worst, thinking their going be executed one by one. They are dragged out of the cage and taken away somewhere for questioning, and no one says anything.

The drink of truth...

A witch who lives in the woods is summoned to the village, forcing them to drink a potion enchanting them into telling her what she wants to know.

Their mouths are forced open, holding them on their knees, whilst the potion is forced into their mouths by the villagers thrown to the ground, with crossbows pointed at him, whilst it takes a short while to take effect on the soldier.

The villagers start asking a lot of questions about what they hear for, how they got here, and what they want.

The strong drug makes the soldiers tell them everything they want to no, seeing them as not attackers who want their village to be released from the cage.

Releasing the soldiers...

They apologise to the soldiers, but they have been under attack a few times already and fear another attack.

All their soldiers were either killed or enslaved at the market by bandits, and their traders that frequented the island lost lots of good soldiers. They are open and easy pickings for the enemy to attack, so they hide in the woods.

Not knowing how skilled the soldiers are, take them under their wing, but its the soldiers that can teach them.

They are very interested in their crossbows technology, preferent to use one them instead of a bow and arrow.

The villagers share their stock of crossbows with them and arming themselves, to set up three camps around a village of ten per camp.

With no way home, the soldiers vow to keep the villagers safe as long as they are there in return for food, drink and a bed to rest in.

Audience with the king...

The next day, they are awakened and taken to the great island tribal king Syla, sat upon a large seat.

They bow down in respect for his authority and status, they are asked to rise up again from the floor.

Introducing themselves to the king, telling him what happened and how they ended up here, by accident blind in the dark.

They go on to tell him about the monster they encountered on the way here and the men they lost.

The king is surprised by the slaying of the water beast, as no weapon can cut threw its body. They have tried to leave before and failed. None of their men or boats have returned back, and they lost a lot of people that way so they fear leaving the island.

The council consists of eight elders picked and voted by the villagers, four on each side of the king.

The elders consist of great warriors in their own right, now too old to fight, who try to train younger villagers. Two of their best-armed village guards are placed at the door inside and outside of the makeshift hut they put together just for this meeting.

With constant attacks, they cannot have a permanent base as enemies will take them prisoner, especially a king and elders.

They stay in hiding, blending in and kept safe in the woods away from attackers' grips, or their civalisation will crumble without them.

Welcoming arms...

Both sides introduce themselves as the soldiers begin to explain how they got here and what they had to overcome.

Welcoming to the village, they are allowed to stay as long as they want as the village has no proper soldiers to defend it.

Everyone, happy and in agreement with the king orders a great feast in their honour with plenty of food and drink.

The king has one more term to teach the villagers how to fight and protect themselves against attackers.

All agreed to continue drinking and eating, enjoying themselves, tomorrow becomes their first day of training.

Friendly combat...

With wooden swords and shields at the ready, the new villagers prepare to train with the soldiers.

After they practice striking against trees, the soldiers divide them into two groups, one attacking with swords and the other defending with shields.

The villagers really start to enjoy themselves. Constantly changing it up makes them swap sides, trading swords for shields.

No way home...

Threw out the enjoyment of training new soldiers, they know there's no way home for them and with every day passing, a bigger hole appears in their hearts.

Knowing they're lost at sea, no matter how much they wanted to go home, even if they were to they wouldnt no which direction to go.

A home away from home...

The village king sees their sorrow and tells them they're welcome on his island for as long as they want to stay.

The king tells them of many new places out there to visit if they don't want to stay, now mercenaries without a home.

The soldiers accept the king's offer, hoping they see a trader they recognise that could take them home one day.

They hold hope in their hearts and go about everyday life in their new home, adjusting the best way they can.

Back at Nestra...

Hope is lost for their fellow villagers. When their soldiers don't return from their overseas incursion with a new trade ally, securing their new home for them, the traders promise to keep their eyes peeled and ears up will help them find them the best they can.

They wait many weeks for their soldiers to return, but none return. Fearing their end, they send the word out to all traders if they have seen them as traders from that region came to trade, they become worried when they dont return with them.

The traders had no idea and told them that they saw them set sail back to the island intact and full of happiness due to a great victory.

Defenceless...

The villagers start to panic as theirs no soldiers left to protect them, as they send all of them out to sea.

Unprotected, the island is vulnerable to foreign attacks for the first time ever, and the gods will only help with supernatural forces.

The villagers no this. All their possessions and even their lives are at risk from outside attackers and slave traders.

They have to replenish their army camps as soon as possible with whoever they can draft into service. The training will be extreme for the new recruits, but with threats on the horizon, it's normal for their lost soldiers.

Training new recruits...

With no soldiers left, all were sent overseas for what would seem to be an easy fight, but none returned. Volunteers soon filled the ranks, remembering their training, and soon started training very hard, not letting up, making their old trainers proud wherever they may be.

As there could be an attack at any time, their training is a lot harder than normal, pushing them to the limit. Having a full artillery of wooden swords and shields, they switch into two groups, violently clashing shields and lacking swords.

The search begins...

A candle flickers in a lantern in the darkness as a lone group of villagers make their way into uncharted waters, setting sail into the unknown. The travellers are wary of their surroundings as they can't see anything in front of them or around them, just the small light on the boat.

Many hours pass, floating along in the darkness, trying to find evidence of their soldiers being there looking for wreckage along the way, anything to give them hope. They come across nothing, just miles of open water, not even a single island around them that they could restock at. They take shifts, keeping watch whilst the rest nap, conserving their energy so their not all tired the next day.

One villager is at the front of the boat, jotting down their course so they don't get lost and are able to find their way back.

Rocky waters...

A storm hits the open sea, sending waves crashing into their boat. As they try to keep it up straight, drenched and cold, they huddle together to try and keep warm with the spare blankets they brought with them.

Food reserves ran low as they expected; they used fishing nets and rods to catch their dinner.

They rashen the water as they can't get anymore, and they no to drink from the ocean would be madness.

The sunrise brings hope...

With the morning sun comes calm waters, able to see they start their journey a lot better rested and ready than the previous night, sailing perfectly on the crystal clear waters as fish can be seen swiming around beneath their boat.

The early sun is warm upon their heads as it rises up from the sea line, sitting up high in the sky bringing about a lovely day to be sailing.

Looking into the water, they can see coral, fish and other creatures that live deep down at the bottom, not a sunken boat or a body in sight. As they continue their journey across the open sea, spirits are high that they might still be alive.

Travelling all night threw bad weather, they realise thier lost now and don't know which way is home anymore.

Pirates descend....

They see small boats in the distance, and they wave them down as the boats come closer and closer. Thinking their saved start to celebrate.

Not knowing what a pirate is being shielded from that on their island, they are very welcoming to the strangers on their ships.

The pirates take them and their boat hostage, taking all their food and goods aboard and stripping them of their valuables and other handheld goods. Very afraid, the villagers don't know what to do as they are tied up and taken aboard their ships, blindfolded, so they don't know where they are going. Many hours pass at sea until they hear noises coming from in front of them, but blindfolded shake in fear of what fate they will meet.

Enslaved.....

Still tied up and blindfolded, they are tossed from the boats they were in onto the beach of a faraway place. They are put in a line where they can hear an auction taking place, unable to see what they are taken away and chucked into a cage.

With their blindfolds off and untied, they see other people locked up with them as well, strangers taken prisoner like they were.

Cost of slaves...

The slave market is bustling with many buyers and sellers, and they line up slaves as the highest bidder wins the slaves.

Slaves disappear quickly as the money comes flowing in from many different slave traders for personal slaves to fulfil their every desire.

With such a high demand, the prison is thinking fast, and they have to do something fast before they end up getting sold on themselves.

Many prisoners were taken, never to be seen again, but some of the servants talked to the prisoners, keeping them up to date with whats going on.

Not wanting to be sold on ending up god knows where, they gather together with the others a devise a plan to escape.

They all would have to play along for the plan to work, allowing them a limited window of opportunity to escape together.

The other prisoners notice the prison is lightlyguarded at night, and that time would be better to escape.

Midnight escape...

The plan is made, and all agree to it. At midnight, they will all escape; not knowing when midnight is, they get a slave to pass by just before.

All is set; as the slave passes by, the rest of the prisoners pretend to be asleep, and one of them is still awake.

The fellow prisoner pretends to collapse on the floor, shaking like crazy as the rest pretend to be asleep. The guards rush in to see what's wrong with the prisoner as the rest jump him from behind. They take their keys and rush out of the village to the shore, where there a boats just lying around. They all run to the boats and push them out to sea, fleeing as fast as they can, rowing their boats.

Back on the high sea...

All scatter in different directions, leaving the villagers to go on their way to find their lost soldiers once again.

Not knowing where they are, speed away, rowing fast from the island, not knowing where they are going putting distance between them and their captures.

The lure of human nature...

As they drift to a nearby island, the singing of beautiful women can be heard from the island, a tune that catches the heart like a fish luring them in.

The closer they get, the more difficult it becomes to resist them until thier nearly at the beach.

Loving embrace...

Making it to the island, they disembark their boats and are surrounded by beautiful women not dressed in much.

They lure the villagers up to their castle with beautiful singing and dancing and smells of delicious food.

One day turns into five years...

They enter a room full of tables of food and drink everywhere as if they were expecting them to arrive.

Partying and eating the food as time flies by outside but freezes inside the castle of the half-naked women who seem to be alone without men's suspicion at first, they think none of it as they start to enjoy themselves dancing with the women and have lots to drink.

Soul suckers...

Lured into a chamber full of human remains, they transform into their true forms, terrifying the villagers. The beautiful women turn into evil creatures in the shape of a human woman, hairy and gruesome drugged from the food. They are almost defenceless as their mouths are forced open, and their souls are slowly sucked out.

Escape before death...

One close to death bearly gets his knife out, stabbing it straight into the heart, killing the creature as it drops him to the floor.

Getting up off the floor quickly charges the remaining monsters sucking the souls from their bodies, running his sword threw their backs and piercing their hearts.

Helping the rest of the villagers up, gather their composure as they head back to their boats to continue on their travels. Entering the room with all the food and drink, to saw only rotten food with maggots and other insects crawling on like they were under a spell.

Almost throwing up, they stagger out the room and head for the boats trying to forget this whole thing ever happened.

Hidden treasures...

Leaving the room, they see a glint in the corner of their eye, going to the room they just passed.

Heading back to the room, curious, they can't believe their eyes at what's staring them in the face.

Entering the room, they notice it packed with gold coins and all sorts of treasure just thrown in for anyone to take. As they grab as much as they can, they hear a terrifying roar come from deep inside the castle. Spooked, they run with their new loot.

Demonic hounds...

Running out as quickly as they can, they're soon chased by black hounds with black gleaming eyes, gaining on them quickly.

Blood-curdling growling can be heard getting closer and closer, filling them with fear as they flee.

Not being able to run very fast with so much treasure in their hands, they drop and scarper to their boats, dragging them into the water.

The demonic hounds don't follow them into the water. They just stop at the water's edge as if they are afraid of the water.

With a weight off their minds as they sail into the distance, blocking out what just happened to them.

Rowing away with a weight off the villagers, thinking they would end up as food, look back as the dogs grow smaller and smaller in the background.

Strangers need help...

Along their journey, they see two turned-over boats with people sitting on the top of them as sharks circle around them.

Very scared of being eaten, they shout out for help as they see the villager's boats coming close; they all celebrate as the boats come ever so closer, scaring off the sharks. As they swim away, never to return, they risk the swim, swimming over to the boats, their boats too damaged to continue on. The villagers offer to take them home, asking them for directions.

Helping the strangers home...

After they reach the boats, the villagers help them up into the boats, pulling one up at a time as they rest hold on the side, giving them blankets to keep warm and to dry in. They give the outsiders all the food and drink they can. They soon dry off under the harsh sunlight. Now recovered, they ask them if they can take them home. The outsiders give them directions to their island, setting sail straight away, happy they visiting a new place they have never been.

Making new friends...

Great for their help and not becoming shark food, introduce them to the locals as they enter the village.

They offer the villagers a bed for the night and as much food and drink as they can consume. The village reminds them a bit of home, and they yearn to return one day. They enjoy themselves.

The next day...

They awake early in the morning, greeted by the locals. They are happy that the villagers helped their people home safe and sound. They are offered new clothes, a bath to clean themselves up, and a hearty breakfast of bread and fresh fish.

The villagers could hear loud cheering coming from the local tavern, so they went to investigate what was going on.

Reaching the tavern they open the door and walk in, and everyone freezes for a few seconds before continuing to drink.

They soon find out it's for the outsiders that were lost, celebrating not being killed at sea and for their safe return.

They take their seat in the tavern as drinks are brought over to them in the biggest mug they ever seen.

Helpful locals...

The locals put out the word to see where their lost villagers could be, passing it on to all traders who visited.

They are having a great time on the island, taking advantage of all the pleasures given to them. In the meantime, as they wait for word of their lost brothers, many traders come and go with no word of where they could be. Frustrated, the villagers try to take their minds off it.

A few weeks later...

Whilst they sleep in a deep slumber, they get a visit in the middle of the night with good news, telling them they have been found.

They will take them first thing in the morning ., telling them to rest up for the long adventure ahead.

Excited that they will be reunited with their lost brothers, I can't sleep just waiting for morning to come.

The morning soon comes as they burst out of their huts and head for the ship; being the only ones there so early, they sit patiently and wait for the locals to come, throwing stones into the water around the boat the locals tie the villager's boats to their ship, tightening them with strong rope so they don't get lost at sea.

Out at sea...

Setting sail as the villagers get more and more excited to see them again, having a lot of questions for them to see what they have been up to.

They grow impatient as the journey is very long and could take all day to get there, so they decide to take a nap to kill some time.

Many hours pass by as they awake near the island where their soldiers are; they jump from the ship and swim fast to the island. Reaching the island, they lay on the beach catching their breath, tired from swimming as fast as they could.

The locals go ahead of them to introduce them to the new villagers, following behind them at pace.

Their lost brother's fount...

They make their way into the village, spotting some people resting by a fire. They can't help themselves, so they shout out to them.

Not recognising them with long hair and beards in simple clothing, hoping they shouted to the right people one looks towards them, not recognising them at first hearing them, recognise who they are and praying for this day for a long time, jump up onto their feet and go hug them.

Introducing them to the villagers and showing them around the village where they have been living for so long.

Introductions....

The soldier introduces them to the king and elders who have been looking after them for such a long time.

The locals welcome them into the village and all its delights but are still content with their other villagers, whom they had refused kindly at first.

The soldiers tell the locals to fetch wine so they can all drink, toasting to being fount only after five long years of waiting, but it went by fast, and now they got a chance to return home to Nestra once again and share their newly gained wisdom and technology.

Some refuse to go home now they have families here and don't want to be a part of them, ask to stay and are granted.

Being sad to leave without them as they have grown very close together over the years, wish them well and give them a hug.

Packing up...

They slowly start to return to their huts to pack up all the things they have accumulated over the years.

Unable to take everything with them, they just take their jewellery and fine clothes along with their crossbows.

The villagers had never seen a crossbow before, and it was completely alien to them. The soldiers tell them it will replace bows and arrows, and they know how to make them.

With everything on board the ship, they set sail to one of Nestra's long-range trade partners.

I told them that one day they would reach Nestra to trade with, but at the moment, they could not make it that far; other boats wouldn't make it.

Reaching the trade post...

With sails up high, the wind carries them to the island of the faraway traders, and they will have to wait till they are out that way again.

The kind locals that dropped them off there gave them enough gold coins to last till their home again. With not much coin to get them home, the soldiers show them how to make deadly crossbows in trade for the journey home. They don't take the trade at first, calling them crazy until one soldier shows them how it works. They are amazed at its power.

A deal is made quickly, showing them how to make them. They take up less room than a normal bow and arrow, an upgrade from a bow and arrow. They throw them all away and quickly mass-produce them for their locals.

Setting sail for home...

Awoken early by the traders, the remaining soldiers and the villagers embark on their final journey to their homeland. Spirits high, they look forward to seeing their own again. Setting foot back on the beaches, hoping they would recognise them, as it's been over five years since they were last here, they become a bit anxious.

Armed soldiers appear from everywhere, surrounding them with swords drawn, not recognising them.

They see them as attackers ready to invade. The elders appear on the beach, and one of them recognises the soldiers.

They tell the new soldiers to lower their weapons and show respect for their once-lost guardians. The elder gives them all a big hug and welcomes them back to Nestra, taking them back to the village.

They shaved them and cut their hair so the other villagers would recognise them, taking them to the local tavern.

New weapons...

After many drinks, they all become very drunk, challenging each other to a target practice competition.

They all collect their bows and arrows as the soldiers return to the beach to collect their goods. Amongst their goods are the very powerful crossbows they have fine-tuned over the years. Taking them out, they accept the challenge. The rest of the competitors look on in disbelief as it doesn't look very powerful compared to their bows and arrows.

A short compertition...

The archers take their positions, choosing their targets. They go for the big, easy ones while the soldiers take on the small ones with their crossbows.

Thinking they haven't got a chance to hit them, they laugh at them as they take aim, pulling their bows back and firing.

They hit the targets perfectly. Now, it's the soldiers' turn. They pull back the crossbows and aim through the site on the crossbow, hitting the targets very easily.

Crossbow production...

Very impressed, they wanted to know how something so powerful could be so small; the soldiers go on to show to to make them and refine them for better performance.

They soon incorporate them into their inventory, mass producing them for everyone to use instead of bows and arrows.

Enough is made for every villager for combat and protection and hunting also from any outside enemys that might attack.

The end of a long day...

The sun sets on another day's end, and everyone puts down their tools and heads to the local tavern for a well-earned drink.

Heading to the local tavern for a drink with the local villagers, something they haven't done for a long time, ready to relax with a mug of ale in their hands, drink the rest of the night away before the villagers head home for relaxation before they go to bed.

Back to business...

Awaking the next day, the soldier return to their posts as if nothing had happened, but they are looking forward to going back to their posts.

Rested and ready for anything, the soldiers line up for inspection by their new commanding officer.

Inspection over, they take up their crossbows and patrol the outskirts of the village, covering all the weak points.

Happy now their back protecting them, the villagers go about their everyday tasks safely in the fact they are protected.

Thanking the gods...

They thank the gods for their soldier's safe return, leaving offerings and other goods on the church altar.

As they hear a series of loud impacts and blood-curdling screaming coming from outside, they rush outside only to see death and destruction. Their fellow villagers who weren't crushed by the meteors were burning to death right in front of their eyes; powerless to help them, they could do nothing else than watch on as they lost their fellow villagers and friends.

Some run to the beach with buckets to try and put out the fire consuming the villagers before it kills them, but by the time it takes to get the water and then take it back to the village again, it takes too long, and the people burn to death.

Escaping the destruction...

Having nowhere to escape, they drag boats down the sandy beach to take cover on the open water, drifting slowly on their boats can only watch the onslaught of the unfortunate villagers who didn't make it to the boats.

Spine-tingling screams can be heard coming from the village as the unlucky few burn to death in the village fires caused by the meteors.

Safe from the onslaught of meteors, they can do nothing but sit and wait for it to be over so they can salvage their belongings.

The village has been totally destroyed, and the villagers are unable to rebuild, so they decide to travel out onto the sea to find a new home.

Leaving the island...

They embark on a new journey out to see as many look forward to the peaceful sail across the open ocean in search of a new home, trying to forget the screams and the smell of burning flesh in their noses, abandoning their homes for pastures new, they look back as the island gets smaller and smaller into the distance, unsure were they going, miss home already.

The end of Nestra...

Lost Forever is a ghost island with only death and destruction in its wake; there is no way back home now it's lost forever.

Once a great island full of lavish goods and plenty of food and drink now desolate, burnt to a crisp and destroyed.

Thinking the gods would save them from the meteor strikes, but they didn't. Turning on the gods, they are soon forgotten.

They say goodbye to the island and set sail for a whole new adventure out at sea, looking forward to their new discoveries.

Having their weapons with them as they carry them everywhere with them are well protected from pirates and other attackers, twenty boats strong full of armed villagers set sail all together, not knowing where they will end up.

The beginning of the sea villagers...

Out on the open sea, the villagers enjoy the great weather as the sun beats down upon their heads.

Now nomads upon the open sea searching for a new place to settle in and call their own, making sure it is safe to live there.

Hungry and thirsty, they try to find somewhere where they can get refreshments. They see a local trader in the distance.

Knowing the traders well, they sail to the island, where they are greeted at the beach, pulling all their boats onto the beach.

Thinking they were all dead as they had not long visited Nestra, and it looked like no one had survived as everything was destroyed.

They are welcoming to the villagers, offering them drink and food and rest by a hot fire. They ask them what happened.

They explain how big rocks fell from the sky destroying the village with destructive force and the following fires caused by them.

A bed for the night...

The traders offer them a bed for the night as at night it can be dangerious out at sea. They could be lost very easily.

A storm approaches the island, and high winds blow as the storm gains momentum. Grateful for the offer, they all retreat inside out of the weather.

As they retreat into the tavern, a lot of drinks are ordered to pass the time until the storm passes by.

Everyone is in good spirits, and they ask them where they're headed. They tell them they're looking for a new home.

The traders knew lots of places where they could stay and settle, and they had many allies who would take them in.

They retire for the night whilst they think about the most generous offer from the traders, they all have a small meeting.

The next day....

They kindly refuse the request as they would prefer to look for themselves, the traders understand.

Giving them some supplies to last them a good few days as they look for a new home out at sea.

Thanking them for their help the villagers go on their way back out onto the sea to resume their search. Sixty people sail away from the island, looking back as the island becomes a dot on the horizon.

Bit of trouble at sea...

Four boats approach them at speed, thinking they're an easy target to get closer and closer. The villagers do not know their pirates.

They come in very close, taking out their swords try to hijack the villagers' boats, but what they don't realise is their all armed.

Surprise attack...

The pirates are mere feet away from them as they all pull out their crossbows, and they freeze in fear.

The villagers notice their ship in the distance and have a plan to take it for themselves, as their boats are no good in a storm.

They take the pirate's prisoner as they make their way to the ship; surprised there's only a Skellington crew, they are taken easily.

Loading their new ship with all their goods from their boats, raise the sail and bring up the anchor.

They leave their boats with the pirates and take the ship for themselves, setting sail into the distance.

Their new ship...

The ship is huge and well-made, capable of carrying them all on a long journey in front of them.

Sailing away decide to check out the ship, not knowing it's full of treasure taken from poor people they have raided.

With enough treasure to last them a long time as they do not know when they will find somewhere perfect to live.

The ship is big enough to carry all sixty villagers instead of being cramped into boats have room to move around.

They are very happy with their new ship, and their spirits are at an all-time high as things are looking up for them. A bit of luck eventually.

The search continues as they travel miles across the ocean at a high speed. The wind is great on the sail, and they are making great time.

Island ahead...

Sailing quickly, they see a small island in front of them in the distance, and they head straight for it at high speed. Reaching the island, they disembarked using the smaller boats attached to the ship. Some stay behind to guard the ship.

A small scouting party reach the island, weapons ready climbs off their boats and heads up the beach and into the woods.

Searching through the woods see no locals anywhere. It looks deserted, with plenty of wildlife to sustain them for a long time.

They send word back to the ship to come in as the island is clear. They bring the ship in as close as possible.

All sixty villagers disembark and bring all their supplies and treasure with them onto the island.

The gods find them....

They hear a loud thunder and a great flash of light blinding them as they turn away, unable to stand it.

All four gods appear in front of them, and the villagers ask why they would let Nestra be destroyed,

They tell them that they could not interfere in an act of nature as it was not allowed by the other gods.

They have been following them threw their adventure, looking after them the best they can, unable to help them.

They saw the death and destruction of Nestra it hurt them deeply not being able to lift a finger to help them.

Building their new village...

The villagers decide to settle here, and they get to work building small huts from tree branches and other materials, setting up a small camp near the beach get a small fire burning to keep themselves warm; they start to feel hungry, a small hunting party heads into the woods looking for food come across a small wild boar, they shoot it with their crossbows.

Preparing it for transportation, cut it into pieces so it's easier to carry back as they make their way to the makeshift village.

They put it on the fire to cook for a while before they eat; in the meantime, they go search for water, giving them flasks to fill.

After a while, they find a water stream. They test the water to ensure it's clean, so they fill up the flasks with as much water as possible.

Night falls...

With it being their first night on the island they take turns guarding the villagers as they sleep.

When suddenly, eerie fog consumes the island, reducing visibility to zero as the villagers panic.

They hear branches on the floor crack as something big walks on them, surrounding them from all sides; waking all the villagers up, they take up arms back to back, facing in all directions as the bosses come closer and closer.

Night terrors...

They come out of the fog, monsters with big teeth and large heads with the bodies of people with long claws and sharp feet. The villagers and the gods fight side by side to rid the island of this evil, and the creatures don't stand a chance.

A great number of evil monsters come out of the fog but are no match for the gods or the villager's weapons; as soon as the last creature dies, the fog lifts, and they can see far again, puzzling then greatly about what just happened.

They go back in their makeshift huts whilst others gaurd them and get some rest after the big battle they just had.

Morning soon comes...

They all wake up early and have a discussion about whether they should stay here or go somewhere else. They can't seem to decide as apart from the evil monsters, it's a nice island and it has everything needed to flourish.

They decide to stay a few extra days to see if the same thing happens again, like the night before.

They ask the gods what to do, but they only say it's up to them where they want to go, so we aren't very helpful, but we will fight with them if it happens again. They disappear in a blinding flash of light again in the same way as they appeared.

Naming their new home, they talk amongst themselves, trying to come to an agreement on what to call it.

They decide to call it the island of hope, a fitting name for the island, as they settle into their new home with the gods on their side again.

Searching the island....

They split into teams as they search the island for raw materials so they can build better homes and mine precious minerals.

Some find clay and straw to make bricks with, using large branches for their roofs, and soon get into the slow production of bricks.

The island is very small. It only takes a day or two to travel all the way around it, and the villagers locate the perfect place to set up a home.

The End